The Clippity-Cloppity Carnival

By Valerie Tripp

Illustrated by Thu Thai

★ American Girl®

Published by American Girl Publishing

18 19 20 21 22 23 24 QP 10 9 8 7 6 5 4 3 2 1

Editorial Development: Jennifer Hirsch
Art Direction and Design: Jessica Rogers
Production: Jeannette Bailey, Caryl Boyer, Kristi Lively, and Cynthia Stiles
Vignettes on pages 88–91 by Flavia Conley

americangirl.com/service

Parents, request a FREE catalog at **americangirl.com/catalog.**
Sign up at **americangirl.com/email**
to receive the latest news and exclusive offers.

For Katharine S. Emmons,
with love

Meet the WellieWishers

The WellieWishers are a group of fun-loving girls who each have the same big, bright wish: to be a good friend. They love to play in a large and leafy backyard garden cared for by Willa's Aunt Miranda.

Willa

Ashlyn

Emerson

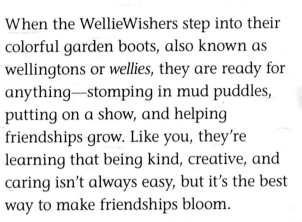

When the WellieWishers step into their colorful garden boots, also known as wellingtons or *wellies*, they are ready for anything—stomping in mud puddles, putting on a show, and helping friendships grow. Like you, they're learning that being kind, creative, and caring isn't always easy, but it's the best way to make friendships bloom.

Camille

Kendall

Chapter 1

Mr. Louie's Farm

The WellieWishers were very excited. Aunt Miranda's neighbor, Mr. Louie, had invited them to visit—and he lived on a *farm*! Mr. Louie's farm was through the woods, across the field, and down the hill from Aunt Miranda's garden.

"I've always wanted to visit Mr. Louie's farm," said Camille.

"Me, too!" said the other girls.

As they skipped along the sunny path, they sang to the tune of "Old MacDonald Had a Farm":

Mr. Louie has a farm, E-I-E-I-O!
And on that farm he has some . . .

"CHICKS!" shouted Willa.

And all the girls sang: *E-I-E-I-O!*

"I sure *hope* Mr. Louie has chicks—
and chickens," said Willa, who loved
birds of all sorts.

"Cock-a-doodle-doo! And some
roosters, too!" rhymed Kendall.

"Egg-zactly!" Willa agreed.

Ashlyn hopped a happy little hop. "I hope Mr. Louie has horses," she said. "I've never met a real horse before!"

"Welcome to my farm," said Mr. Louie.

"Thank you for inviting us," said the girls.

"Your farm is *won*derful!" exclaimed Emerson, spinning and flinging her arms open wide. "I *love* it."

"There's something for *everyone* to love on a farm," said Mr. Louie.

Mr. Louie was right!

Willa loved the clucking hens, crowing roosters, and—best of all—the brand-new flock of peeping, cheeping chicks!

Kendall loved the tractor. Mr. Louie let her sit on the seat and pretend to drive, while he explained how the tractor worked.

Camille loved filling the splishy-splashy water trough for a thirsty mother cow and her baby calf.

Emerson loved the woolly-haired sheep and lambs. She could see that the sheep were confused but amused when she sang to the tune of "Mary Had a Little Lamb":

Hello, woolly sheep and lamb,
Sheep and lamb, sheep and lamb!
Hello, woolly sheep and lamb,
My name is Emerson.

Ashlyn loved looking at Mr. Louie's horse. It had long, strong legs and a dark, shiny coat. It looked very peaceful as it grazed in a far corner of the pasture.

"That horse is so far away that I can hardly see it," complained Emerson. She waved and hollered, "Yoo-hoo! Horsie! Yoo-hoo!"

The horse lifted its head and turned to face the girls. "Oh, look!" said Ashlyn, enchanted. "The horse has a streak of white on its nose."

"It looks like a bolt of lightning," said Kendall.

"I wish the horse would come closer," said Ashlyn.

"Here, horsie, horsie, horsie!" called Kendall. "Come!"

But the horse ignored Emerson and went back to grazing.

After a while, Kendall said, "I'm going to try the barn swing."

"Me, too," said Emerson. "Are you coming, Ashlyn?"

"Yes, in a minute," said Ashlyn.

After the other girls left, Ashlyn gazed at the horse, thinking: *I don't blame you for not coming over. Those girls were awfully noisy, weren't they? Maybe you'll come if I whistle softly.*

Softly and sweetly, Ashlyn whistled, *"Whee-oh-wheet."*

The horse lifted its head, pricked up its ears, and looked across the field at Ashlyn.

Ashlyn held out the bunch of carrots. "These are for you," she said.

Then she held her breath, because the horse began to trot, *clip-clop,* over to the fence.

At last, at last, I'm going to meet a real horse! Ashlyn thought.

Clip-clop, clippity-cloppity, clippity-cloppity! Faster and faster and *faster* the horse trotted. Then it began to gallop across the pasture. Dirt and grass flew up behind its hooves. As the horse thundered closer to the fence, it grew bigger, and bigger, and bigger.

"Whoa," croaked Ashlyn, shrinking back.

Whip, the horse switched its tail.

Snork, it snorted its nose.

Stomp, it pawed the ground with its hooves.

Then, *snatch*! The horse stretched its neck way over the fence and grabbed half of the carrots out of Ashlyn's hands with its long yellow teeth.

"Help!" yelped Ashlyn. She tossed the rest of the carrots over the fence and took off running as fast as she could, thinking: *A real horse is really scary!*

When it was time to leave, the WellieWishers thanked Mr. Louie and waved good-bye.

"Oh," sighed Emerson happily. "Wasn't the farm *won*derful? I loved the sheep the best."

"I loved the tractor," said Kendall.

"I loved the chickens," said Willa.

"I loved the watering trough," said Camille.

"I know what you loved best, Ashlyn," said Kendall.

"THE HORSE!" shouted Kendall, Emerson, Willa, and Camille all together.

"Well," Ashlyn began in a wobbly voice.

But Emerson talked over her. "Did the horse ever come closer?" she asked.

Ashlyn shivered, remembering how scary it was when the horse stampeded toward her and snatched the carrots with its long yellow teeth. She was afraid she might cry if she tried to speak. She didn't want to be a scaredy-cat crybaby, so she just nodded.

"Lucky you," said Kendall. "You saw the horse up close!"

Too close, thought Ashlyn.

Emerson began to sing to the tune of "Old MacDonald Had a Farm," and the other girls all joined in, singing at the top of their voices:

Mr. Louie has a farm,
E-I-E-I-O!

Ashlyn didn't sing, but she made up her own words inside her head:

And on his farm he has a horse.
Is the horse nice? NO!

Chapter 2

Horsing Around

The next day, Camille ran into the garden. "Look, look, *look*!" she shouted. She held out a box that had five small plastic horses in it. "My big brother says he's too old to play with these anymore, so he gave them to me," she said. "We can each have one."

"Thanks, Camille!" said the rest of the girls.

"Ashlyn, you choose first because you like horses the best of all of us," said Camille generously.

"Which plastic horse are you going to pick?" Kendall asked Ashlyn.

"I choose the white horse," said Ashlyn.

The little plastic horse fit in Ashlyn's hand. It wasn't scary at all, not like Mr. Louie's real horse.

The WellieWishers liked their little plastic horses so much that they went horse crazy. They played with them all the time. There was nothing they loved more than horsing around with

their horses! Most of all, they liked
to pretend that their horses were real.
They let them eat grass, like real
horses do.

The girls read books and watched movies about horses. They drew pictures of horses. They sang songs about horses. Willa sang "Yankee Doodle." Ashlyn sang a lullaby.

Yankee Doodle went to town, a-riding on a pony.

Go to sleep, my little baby. When you wake, you shall have all the pretty little horses.

Kendall sang "Over the River and Through the Wood." Camille sang "Jingle Bells." And Emerson sang, "She'll Be Comin' Round the Mountain."

Oh what fun it is to ride in a one-horse open sleigh!

The horse knows the way to carry the sleigh through the white and drifted snow!

She'll be driving six white horses when she comes!

"Let's name our horses," suggested Camille. "I'm going to call mine Giant because if it were real, it would be big and strong."

"I'm going to call my horse Power Pony," said Emerson, "because it would be powerful."

"Mine's Tornado," said Kendall. "A tornado is wild."

"My horse is Cheetah," said Willa. "Cheetahs are super fast, like horses." She asked Ashlyn, "What are you going to name your horse?"

"Snowflake," answered Ashlyn.

"Snowflake is a pretty name," said

Camille, "but don't you think it sounds more like the name of a little bitty kitten than a big strong horse?"

"You should call your horse Blizzard," suggested Kendall.

"No," said Ashlyn. "Snowflake likes the name Snowflake."

"Ohh-kay," shrugged the other girls.

"Let's make a stable for our horses," said Kendall. "We can use the box they came in."

The WellieWishers divided the box into stalls. In each stall, they put a little pile of grass and pretended it was hay for their horses to eat. They filled tiny cups with water for their horses to drink. Ashlyn put a pink silk pillow in Snowflake's stall.

"Don't you think that silky pink pillow looks more like a bed for a princess than a horse?" asked Kendall.

"A horse doesn't sleep in a bed, anyway," said Willa.

"Especially not a pink silk bed," added Emerson. "It would get all dirty and smelly."

Camille handed Ashlyn an old scrap of cloth. "Horses *do* have blankets. Use this rag."

"No, thanks," said Ashlyn. "Snowflake likes the pink silk pillow."

"Ohh-kay," shrugged the other girls.

"Let's pretend our horses are wild ponies stampeding across the prairie," said Emerson.

Clippity, cloppity! With their plastic horses in their hands, the girls galloped and whinnied. They stomped their feet and tossed their heads.

Ashlyn spun on one foot. She hummed a pretty tune and made Snowflake spin on one hoof.

"That's nice," said Willa, "but you're making Snowflake dance like a ballerina instead of stampeding like a wild pony."

"And stampeding ponies are *noisy*," said Kendall. "You should snort and whinny and neigh, like this: *NEIGH-AY-AY-AY!*"

"No, thanks," said Ashlyn. "Snowflake is quiet and graceful."

"Ohh-kay," shrugged the other girls.

The girls watched Ashlyn put Snowflake to bed.

"You keep Snowflake so clean and perfect," said Emerson. "Don't you want to make her more like a *real* horse?"

"No," said Ashlyn. "I like her the way she is."

A Carnival!

It's fun to pretend that our plastic horses are real," said Kendall.

"Yes," agreed Willa. "But it was even *more* fun to see real animals at Mr. Louie's farm."

"I bet other kids would like to see real animals, like we did," said Camille. "Let's ask Mr. Louie to bring some farm animals here to the garden, and invite our friends and families to come see them."

"Oh, that's a great idea!" said Willa. "And we could have other fun things for our guests to do, too, like games to play—"

"And food to eat," said Ashlyn.

"And I'll put on a puppet show!" said Emerson, clapping her hands with glee.

"It will be a carnival," said Kendall.

"A carnival!" cheered all the girls. "Hooray!"

Aunt Miranda said it was fine for the girls to have a carnival. She called Mr. Louie, and he said he'd be glad to bring a lamb and some chickens to the garden.

The girls went right to work to get ready for their carnival. Willa set up a beanbag toss game. Camille set up a cotton candy machine. Ashlyn made a list of things that needed to be done.

Kendall built a puppet stage. Emerson made puppets and planned a puppet show. Carrot wanted to be in the puppet show, too!

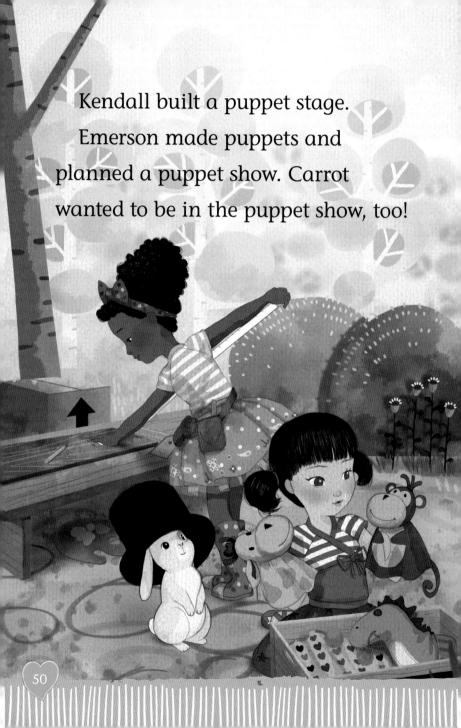

Aunt Miranda came by. "My!" she said. "You girls are working hard on your carnival. Good for you!"

"We want everyone to have fun," said Camille.

"They're going to *love* the real animals," said Emerson. "They'll think the real animals are *won*derful."

"They'll love them best of all, just like we do," said Willa.

"I'm sure they will," said Aunt Miranda.

Aunt Miranda left for a moment. But soon she was back. "Good news!" she said, with a big, bright smile. "I called Mr. Louie again. I told him how excited you are about having real animals at your carnival, and he said that as a special treat he's going to bring a horse."

Willa, Kendall, Camille, and Emerson shrieked with joy. They hopped up and down and hugged each other.

Oh, no, thought Ashlyn, horrified. *That scary horse is coming here?*

Aunt Miranda said, "Mr. Louie will lead his horse around the garden, and you and the kids who come to your carnival can take turns having rides. The horse's name is Thunderstorm."

Thunderstorm? Ashlyn thought. She felt as though she had thunder in her stomach and her hair was standing straight on end like lightning bolts coming out of her head.

"Thunderstorm!" exclaimed the other girls delightedly.

"We saw Mr. Louie's horse when we visited his farm," said Kendall. "It was dark gray like a thundercloud all over, except for a white streak on its nose that looked like lightning. Thunderstorm is the perfect name for Mr. Louie's horse."

"And Thunderstorm will be right *here,* in our garden, at our carnival," sighed Emerson, clasping her hands together.

"And we'll get to ride him," said Willa. "How exciting!"

After Aunt Miranda left, Emerson turned to Ashlyn. "You must be the happiest of all, Ashlyn," she said. "You've already met Thunderstorm, haven't you?"

"Yes," said Ashlyn. The other girls were so pleased and excited. How could she talk them out of inviting that awful horse to their carnival?

Ashlyn took a deep breath and said, "I don't think it's a good idea to bring a horse into our garden. It'll stomp on the flowers, and tear the leaves off branches, and pull up clumps of grass. It'll scare Carrot. And big horses scare little kids, too. You don't know what a real horse is like."

"We've read a lot about real horses," said Emerson. "So we do know a lot about them."

"Well, I'm the only one here who's actually *met* a real horse!" Ashlyn said, snatching Snowflake away from Kendall. She stamped her foot. "I'm tired of you all thinking that you know more than I do about horses!" she said furiously. "That's it! I am NOT coming to the carnival."

"What?" wailed Willa. "We can't do the carnival without you."

"It won't be any fun if you aren't there," said Kendall. "We'll miss you so much."

"And you'll miss my puppet show," added Emerson, waving the puppets at

Ashlyn, who turned away and started
to leave.

"Please, Ashlyn!" Camille called
after her. "Wait."

But it was too late. Ashlyn had
stormed off.

Chapter 4

Chicken

Camille found Ashlyn crying by the garden gate. Without saying a word, Camille sat next to Ashlyn and waited for her to stop crying.

"I'm sorry for stamping my foot and storming off," snuffled Ashlyn.

"I'm sorry we were bossy about horses," said Camille.

"That's not the real reason I don't want to come to the carnival," Ashlyn confessed.

"It's not?" asked Camille.

Ashlyn shook her head. "The real reason is that I'm afraid of Mr. Louie's horse, Thunderstorm," she said.

"You are?" asked Camille. "How come?"

"At the farm, after the other girls had left, Thunderstorm stampeded straight at me," Ashlyn explained. "He galloped so fast that I was afraid he'd break down the fence and crush me." Ashlyn acted out for Camille all the terrible things Mr. Louie's horse had done. "He whipped his tail and snorted his nose and stomped his feet and snatched the carrots right out of my hands with his huge yellow teeth."

"Yikes," shuddered Camille. "That *does* sound scary."

Ashlyn sighed. "The truth is that I don't want to come to the carnival because I'm scared of that horse," she said, looking shamefaced. "I guess I'm a chicken."

"Everybody's afraid of *something*," said Camille. "Take me, for instance. I'm scared of snakes. Snakes are what *I'm* chicken about. *Cluck, cluck.*"

Ashlyn smiled a small smile.

"Anyway," Camille went on, "after the way Mr. Louie's horse acted, you have good reason to be afraid of it. And you know what? I'll tell you a secret: My mom bought those little plastic horses to help my brother get over his fear of horses. It worked. He doesn't need the plastic horses anymore. That's why he gave them to me."

"Really?" said Ashlyn. She was beginning to feel better.

Camille put her arms around Ashlyn. "When Thunderstorm comes, I'll hold your hand and stay right by you all the time," she said. "You won't need to go near him."

"Promise?" asked Ashlyn.

"Promise," said Camille. "Okay?"

Ashlyn nodded slowly. "Ohh-kay,"
she said.

Chapter 5

A Horse of a Different Color

On the day of the carnival, Ashlyn and Camille walked into the garden together.

"You came, Ashlyn! Hooray!" cheered Emerson and Kendall.

"We're so glad you changed your mind," said Willa.

Just then, Mr. Louie drove up in his truck, which had a big horse trailer hitched to it.

Camille stood right next to Ashlyn, as she had promised that she would. She held Ashlyn's hand as Mr. Louie opened the back door and stepped into the horse trailer. "Come on out and meet the girls, Thunderstorm," he said.

Ashlyn gasped. The horse Mr. Louie was leading wasn't scary at all! It was much smaller than the horse that had galloped at her and snatched the carrots from her at the farm.

"That's *Thunderstorm*?" she asked.

"Yup," said Mr. Louie. He patted the pony's rump. "I named her Thunderstorm because of these gray spots shaped like thunderclouds on her rump."

"We thought you were going to bring the big black horse that Ashlyn saw in your pasture," Camille told Mr. Louie.

"The one with the lightning stripe on its nose," added Kendall.

"You mean Flash?" asked Mr. Louie. "No, Flash is too high-strung and skittish to be at your carnival."

"I'll say!" Ashlyn whispered to Camille.

"The day you girls came to the farm, Thunderstorm was far away in the upper pasture, and that's why you didn't see her," Mr. Louie explained. He smoothed Thunderstorm's mane and straightened her bow. "Thunderstorm's a sweetie. You can pet her if you want to."

The WellieWishers hesitated. None of them had ever touched a real horse before, and they were a little nervous—even with a calm, gentle pony like Thunderstorm.

"You go first, Ashlyn," said Camille. She smiled. "You know the most about real horses."

Bravely, Ashlyn reached out and stroked Thunderstorm's nose. It was soft, and the pony's long whiskers tickled Ashlyn's hand.

Thunderstorm pricked her ears toward Ashlyn and looked at her with big soft eyes.

When all the other girls rushed forward at once to pet her, Thunderstorm took a step back.

"I think she's a little scared when you crowd around her like that," explained Ashlyn. She understood how Thunderstorm felt; she knew

all about being scared! "Maybe just pet her one or two at a time."

"I guess even a pony named Thunderstorm can be a little bit chicken at first," said Camille. She and Ashlyn shared a smile.

The WellieWishers' families and friends had a wonderful time at the carnival. The children laughed at Kendall and Emerson's puppet show. They clapped and clapped when Carrot popped out of the top hat.

They oohed and ahhed at the baby
chicks, and they giggled when one
chick sat on Willa's head!

Ashlyn taught kids how to play the beanbag game.

And all the kids ate lots of Camille's cotton candy.

But everyone's favorite part was riding Thunderstorm. Ashlyn rode her THREE times! *Clippity, cloppity, clippity, cloppity, clippity, cloppity!*

When the carnival was over and it was time for the animals to go back to the farm, the WellieWishers said, "Thank you, Mr. Louie!"

"It was very nice of you to bring the lamb and chickens and Thunderstorm to our garden," said Kendall. "You and Thunderstorm *especially* made our carnival so much fun."

"I'm sad to see Thunderstorm leave," said Emerson. "I *love* her. She's *won*derful!"

The girls petted and hugged Thunderstorm one last time. Then they called out, "Good-bye!"

Thunderstorm swished her tail good-bye to all the girls. But Ashlyn was sure that Thunderstorm pricked her ears only toward *her*.

After the carnival, the WellieWishers cleaned up.

"There!" said Willa. "The garden is back to normal now."

"Yes," said Emerson, sounding a tiny bit sad.

No one said anything else for a moment. Then Camille said, "You know, it's funny. I still like our plastic horses, but now that we've had a real pony and a lamb and chickens visit, I wish we could have more animals here in the garden all the time."

"Me, too!" said the other girls.

"Yes," agreed Ashlyn. "But what sort of animals?"

Willa began, " How about—"

"CHICKENS!" her friends finished for her. "We know that you love them!"

"We could build a chicken coop," said Kendall.

Emerson sang to the tune of "Old MacDonald Had a Farm":

In our garden we'll have chicks,
E-I-E-I-O.

"I guess we've all had enough horsing around for a while," joked Ashlyn. "Now we're going to *wing it* with chickens."

"*Egg*-zactly!" said Camille.

Building Bravery

When a child is worried about something, she often finds ways to avoid the situation. She might create distractions, such as picking a fight, creating drama, or feeling sick. She might find excuses ("I didn't want to do that anyway"), procrastinate, or even pretend that there's no problem.

The relief she feels by avoiding her fear rewards the avoidance behavior and encourages it. But while avoidance may make her feel better for a while, the worry or fear doesn't go away; in fact, it can grow more unmanageable the more she avoids the problem. This is because she is teaching herself that the fear is too big to be overcome and can only be avoided. She is convincing herself that she is helpless, rather than proving to herself that she's not!

Take It One Step at a Time

One way to help your child manage a fear is to create scenarios that enable her to perform small acts of bravery. These scenarios will slowly expose your child to the feared situation so that she learns to manage her worry one step at a time. She can begin the process by doing something that scares her only a little bit.

In the story, Ashlyn starts by imagining that her toy horse is gentle and calm and quiet. This helps her feel a little more comfortable about horses in general, though not enough to feel prepared to meet Thunderstorm. For that, she needs the extra support and encouragement of a trusted friend, Camille.

Finally, when the dreaded moment arrives, Ashlyn discovers that she feels empathy with Thunderstorm: She realizes that the pony is a little bit afraid of the girls—a fear that Ashlyn can relate to! Identifying and empathizing with the pony helps her feel more confident and less fearful. Here are some ways to help your child practice being brave until it feels natural.

Make a Bravery Path

Help your child make a list of actions related to her fear.

Ashlyn's list might look like this:

- Look at pictures of horses
- Play with toy horses
- Visit a farm or stable where horses live.
- Stand across the fence or stall door from a horse.
- Pet a horse.
- Ride a horse, led by an adult, for a walk.

Next, ask your child to arrange that list of fears from least scary to most scary. On a large piece of paper or poster board, draw a winding path with stepping stones or sidewalk squares. At the start of the path, write the action that your child finds least scary. Continue writing actions in order along the path. As she faces these smaller fears one at a time, she will gain the confidence to move on to the next step on the Bravery Path. Reward her progress along the path with stickers or stars.

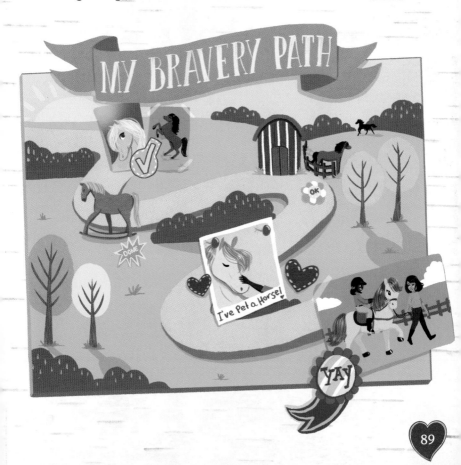

Act It Out

It's important to show your child that you understand her fears while gently demonstrating that they're largely a product of her imagination. Role-playing can be a fun way to do this.

Say your child is afraid of dogs. Start the role-playing game by letting her play the dog while you play a scared child. Not only will this empower her to be "in charge" of the scenario that scares her, but it will also allow you to see precisely what she fears will happen when she encounters a dog. Model the right way to say hello to a dog: Ask the imaginary owner if the dog is friendly and whether it's okay to pet it; then gently reach out your hand to let the "dog" sniff it before petting the "dog" on the shoulder or back.

When it's your turn to be the dog, act out being a happy, friendly dog that wants to be petted. (You can also recruit a sibling for the dog role!) Remind your girl of the gentle steps you took to greet the dog, and give her positive feedback the way a dog would by pretending to wag your tail or maybe rolling over on your back to let her rub your belly.

(It's fine to be silly while role-playing! Laughter helps to relax her and diffuse the fear.)

Make Up a Mantra

Help your child come up with a positive phrase that she can sing or say to herself whenever she's feeling afraid. It's best to choose a simple phrase to memorize and repeat several times a day so that she can remember it easily when she needs it most. Here are a few examples:

About the Author

VALERIE TRIPP says that she became a writer because of the kind of person she is. She says she's curious, and writing requires you to be interested in everything. Talking is her favorite sport, and writing is a way of talking on paper. She's a daydreamer, which helps her come up with her ideas. And she loves words. She even loves the struggle to come up with just the right words as she writes and rewrites. Ms. Tripp lives in Maryland with her husband.

Here are some more WellieWisher books to read!

The Riddle of the Robin

A robin has moved into the garden, thrilling the WellieWishers with its pretty songs. When the girls bring it presents, they learn what robins like to eat. (Hint: It's sort of like spaghetti!) Then one day, the robin disappears. The girls go on a hunt to find it—and get a major surprise! Can animal-lover Willa figure out what's up with her new feathered friend?

Ashlyn's Unsurprise Party

Ashlyn is throwing a party! She wants to keep everything top secret so that she can surprise her friends. Then she learns that her friends have allergies and other needs. At first, Ashlyn is disappointed about letting her friends in on her secret plans—but it turns out that Ashlyn is in for the biggest surprise of all!

The Muddily-Puddily Show

The WellieWishers are putting on a show, and Emerson is in charge. The girls love her songs and silly skits, but not all of Emerson's creative ideas are working. Ashlyn can't see out of her pumpkin costume, Willa has a touch of stage fright, and Kendall is struggling with the special effects. When the girls try to tell her their problems, Emerson doesn't listen. Will the show go on?

Camille's Mermaid Tale

Camille loves the ocean—the warm sand, the pretty shells, and the sparkling waves that tickle her toes. Sometimes she even imagines that she's a mermaid with whales and dolphins for friends! When the other WellieWishers see how much Camille misses her summers by the sea, they want to help . . . but how can four girls turn a garden into an ocean?

The Rainstorm Brainstorm

It's Aunt Miranda's birthday! The WellieWishers want to give her something special, but they can't agree on what it should be. Then Kendall discovers the Tomorrow Pile. What looks like a bunch of old, dirty, broken things to the other girls looks like cool stuff with lots of potential to Kendall! Can the girls use it to make something wonderful?

The Mystery of Mr. E

There's a new friend in the garden—a big, shaggy dog with the mysterious name of Mr. E! The dog loves to play, so when it suddenly disappears, the WellieWishers are worried. They search high and low and find paw prints, but no dog. What has happened to Mr. E? The WellieWishers are about to get the surprise of their life!